... just one more

A book of children's rhymes by

John Trembath

Illustrated by Steve Vardy

ISBN: 978-0-244-80437-4

All profits will go to The Little Harbour Children's Hospice near St. Austell in Cornwall which gives much needed assistance to children and families in the Southwest coping with short and precious lives.

PublishNation
www.publishnation.co.uk

...just one more

Here are some stories
That have to be told.
'Bout Wizards and Dormice,
And wise Owls of old.
You'll meet Edward the Elf,
(Such a naughty young man)
But who tries to be good,
Do the best that he can.

These stories I hope
You will really enjoy.
The words all in rhyme,
That I've had to employ.
So sit back and read them,
Or listen instead
Before you are tucked up
Each night in your bed.

SV19

"Oswald the Owl"

Oswald the Owl is a clever old bird.
Shall I tell you a story about him I heard?
A tale of what happened a long time ago,
When Oswald was young. That I think you should know.

When Oswald was hatched from his egg in the nest,
He looked very strange. No, not quite at his best.
His Mother said "Oh! What an odd chick I've got.
Look! Only three feathers, that isn't a lot.

"I thought he'd be pretty, my first little child.
He looks rather glum, I thought baby chicks smiled!
His eyes are too large, his 'To-Whoo' isn't right,
I don't think my dear baby chick is too bright!!

Poor Oswald. He thought to himself "When I grow,
I'm going to learn all the things Owls should know.
I'm going to learn how to read, how to spell,
I might even learn how to add up as well!"

"But first" our Owl said looking up at the sky,
"I'll have to find out about learning to fly.
I'll just flap my wings, then I'll hop up and down ..."
When suddenly, Whoosh! He was off, skyward bound.

His very first lesson. He did it so well.
The other Owls said "He'll be wise. We can tell.
He'll soon go to school, be the top of his class!"
And that's how it was. How it all came to pass.

He did all his homework, he read every book.
He wrote very neatly, what care Oswald took.
The teachers all said he's the wisest by far.
And pinned on his chest the top prize. A gold star.

He learned and he learned about 'most everything.
Taught Owls how to hoot, and taught Skylarks to sing.
He knew all the rules of the forest by heart.
Could warn when cold winter was going to start.

He solved every problem his friends ever had.
They went away happy, so happy and glad
That Oswald the Owl with such wisdom was blessed.
Could answer each question, Could pass every test.

Now, if you would like to be clever like him,
I'll tell you a place where you have to begin.
You must learn to read, 'cos as Oswald would say
"Be sure you make your way to school EVERY DAY!!

"Prickly Times"

Henry the hedgehog awoke with a start.
It wasn't too early, it wasn't too dark.
So he got out of bed, and he said "Goodness me!
I'll just brush my bristles, and brew up some tea"

"I fancy some apple for breakfast with bread.
A nice juicy one, with a skin rosy red"
But opening the larder door, Ca-tras-to-phe!!
No sign of an apple in there did he see.

Only some wrinkled up skin on the shelf,
And one lonely pip. All alone by itself.
"I thought I had been to the market" he said.
"I'm certain. `Twas just before I went to bed!"

"I'll have to go out, do some shopping somewhere.
Like Old Mother Hubbard, my cupboard is bare
Now, a tin of dried beetle, some nice juicy worms,
That'll do for my breakfast soon as I return"

"Oh, I hope it's not chilly this morning, you see,
These cold autumn days and I just don't agree.
My coat, although spikey, is now rather worn.
Oh, were I a rabbit. Then I would be warm"

Henry the hedgehog prepared to go out.
He wiggled his nose (what some folk call a snout)
Then, opening the door, very slowly at first
He peeped at the sky. Really fearing the worst.

"Those grey autumn days are so dreary" he sighed.
"Who wants to go out when its cosy inside."
But looking again, in the way that you do,
Henry saw that the sky wasn't grey, but bright blue!

No gold fallen leaves were now scattered around;
But primroses, daises, now covered the ground.
Hard to believe that the sun was now warm,
Hard to believe there was no howling storm.

"Magic has happened" he cried with delight.
And all of this took place in one single night.
It's Willie the Wizard, a spell he has spread.
This happened last night. Yes. Whilst I was in bed"

"What rubbish!" a voice came from top of the tree.
Twas Oswald the Owl. He said "Listen to me.
You went fast asleep last October no less.

And while you were snoring,
the world has progressed."

"We've finished with winter, we're now into spring,
With all of the pleasures that that always brings.
Glad that you're back from your slumbers, that's great.
Oh, would that we all could like you ... HIBERNATE.

SV19

"A Gnome's Home"

Hello, I am a Garden Gnome.
This lovely garden is my home.
Here I sit for hours and hours
Admiring all the plants and flowers.

They say I am a gorgeous Gnome,
Who treats this garden as his own!
Telling Butterflies and Bees
'Now don't disturb me, if you please'

'Let me drowse the days away
While waters from the fountain play.
Let me dream, and let me be.
You would! If you're a Gnome, like me.

I first came here some years ago.
A little girl and boy I know
Placed me down, to rest awhile
Because they liked my friendly smile.

And so I sat, and simply stayed.
They quite forgot me I'm afraid.
As time passed by, they grew and grew!
But me? I stayed quite small. Like you.

Some people laugh, and point, and sneer,
Say 'Who's this funny chap sat here?'
But we know Gnomes bring luck, don't we.
That's why they won't get rid of me.

"Hats Off"

Edward the Elf, such a smart little chap
In his coat of bright green, and a red baseball cap.
A red baseball cap? That's not proper or right!"
The King of the Elves said "You look such a sight."

"You know I prefer you in Robin Hood green.
The loveliest colour, so cool and serene.
Oh, if you appear in a red baseball cap,
You'll ruin our style. Where's the logic in that!"

But Edward was stubborn, quite naughty in fact.
He screamed and he shouted. Good manners he lacked.
"I hate my old hat, and as you all know well
I won't wear a hat with a ring-a-ding-bell!!"

Disgraceful behaviour. And in front of the King.
The worst that the world of the Elves had e're seen.
Not liking a hat with a bell on the top?
It's all part of Elf uniform. Yes. Is it not?

But he threw his old hat on the floor in a rage.
With reason or sense Edward wouldn't engage.
No question of trying to talk this thing through,
For Edward, a bell on his hat wouldn't do!

"I want to be modern. I want to be smart.
A red baseball cap will do well for a start.
I want to be cool. Yes, cool, that's what I lack.
Cool guys wear their cap with the peak at the back!"

"The peak at the back??" Cried the King. "Dearie me.
I can't see what use to an Elf that would be.
It certainly won't keep the sun from his eyes.
So is it quite practical!? Is it quite wise?"

"Now maybe the colour is not the main thing.
But bells are important. They give a loud ring.
And what use is a peak that is worn at your back?
It's stupid. It's silly. And that's a known fact."

But Edward the Elf was a crafty young man.
He said "Sire, the reason is part of the plan.
The plan is quite clear. yes, I've checked, *double-checked.*
IT KEEPS THE RAIN OFF FROM THE BACK OF YOUR NECK!

That did it. The King was impressed, so I'm told.
No more would his Elves be off work with a cold.
And as for the bell? Well, I've heard, and it's true,
Now Elves wear a bell fixed to EACH OF THEIR SHOES.

"Bees Please"

It really had been
The most tiring of days.
And Barrie the bee
Seemed to hear his wings say

"We've flown you for miles
Going round and around,
Oh please, won't you find us
Some place to sit down."

So Barrie looked out
For a suitable spot
By checking on Google,
He was certain he'd got

A nice leaf to land on,
There under a tree.
But as he zoomed in,
He exclaimed "Goodness me!"

"Oh, there is that horrid boy
Edward the Elf.
The one who is always
So full of himself.

He loves swatting flies,
Setting bees in a spin,
Will declare to the world
That we'll give him a sting!"

But as he drew closer
He saw with surprise
That Edward the Elf
Had big tears in his eyes.

Was snivelling, and sniffing,
And said with a croak
"I'm really not well.
Got a nasty sore throat."

Then, quick as a flash
Barrie knew what to do.

He said as he settled,
"Now, if I were you
I'd go home to bed,
Drink hot honey, and then
I'd know by the morning
I'd be better again"

Well! Taking his dinner pack
Off from his back,
He handed to Edward
That honey filled pack.

And that kindly deed
Was the starting you see,
Why Edward the Elf
Is more kindly to Bees.

SV19

"Oswald the Great"

Oswald the owl, as I'm sure you have heard
Is renowned as the wisest of all of the birds.
No chattering chaffinch, or parrot that squawks
Can compare to the wisdom that old Oswald talks.

He knows every subject so far known to man.
Can speak every language, Chinese, Hindustan.
A fountain of knowledge, that flows easily,
From that clever old owl sitting up in a tree.

Learned professors, and leaders of state
All stand in line, and they patiently wait
For Oswald to meet them. To greet them, and say
"You're doing it wrong. You should do it this way!"

"Just face the problem, be clear in the mind.
That is the first rule for 'solving' I find.
Nothing's impossible. Let's get that clear"
Then, tapping his forehead he said "It's up here!"

Oswald the owl is a great friend of mine.
Up there in the branches, well, most of the time.
But if it gets stormy, giving cause for alarm,
Then he heads off back home, to his barn, on the farm.

So if a dilemma zooms into your life.
That's causing you trouble, that's causing you strife,
Just pop round to Oswald's, he'll sort it. You'll see.
He'll fix all your troubles, well, he fixed 'em for me.

"Whether the weather"

I'm sure you've heard stories
'Bout Edward the Elf.
Who's not very good
At behaving himself.
He tries very hard,
But the reason you see
Is his 'good' and his 'bad'
Never seem to agree!

Now, Edward's in charge
Of the weather I'm told.
Decides when it's warm,
And decides when it's cold.
So if he's been good,
Well, it's sunny and hot.
But if he's been bad?
Then it's certainly not.

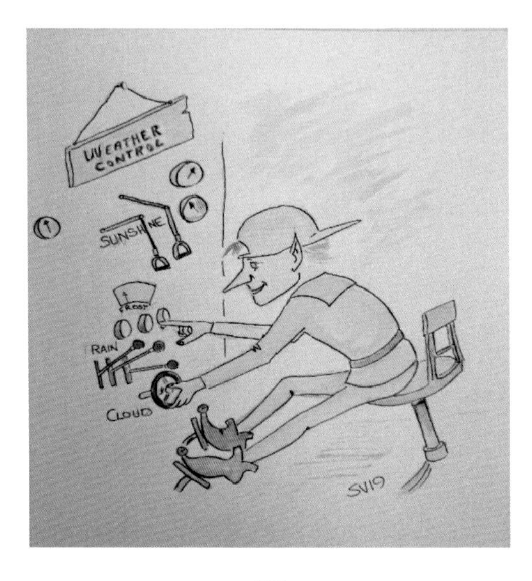

His good, and his bad
Are at war all the time.
Being bad brings on thunder,
The good brings the shine.
But when Edward is caught
Mixing up all this power,
And is just even-tempered,
We call that 'a shower'

So next time you're out
And get caught in the rain
Or it's snowing, or blowing,
The reason is plain.
It's Edward the Elf,
As I've tried to explain,
It's Edward the Elf
Being naughty again!

"That Dratted Denzil"

In a land far away that is known to but few
Lived a bad tempered Dragon, a friend of mine knew.
This Dragon named Denzil, lived in a deep cave
Where no-one would venture. Not even the brave.

Twas said that this Dragon shot flames from his nose.
A strange sort of happening. You know, I suppose
That playing with fire can be dangerous too.
I'm glad that *your* nose wouldn't know what to do!

But Denzil the dragon would give a loud roar,
And bang with his tail on his cave dwelling floor.
Rattling the windows, and chimney-pots too.
Shoot flames from his nose. Oh dear, what a to-do.

The people that lived in the town down below
Were frightened of Denzil, they never did know
When he would come down, and storm through the street.
Shouting and snarling at people he'd meet.

So what are these poor frightened souls going to do?
They'd called in the Army, the Navy, but who
Was bravest amongst them without any doubt
To face this fierce dragon, and put his fire out.

Not one said "I'll go, and live up to my name
As bravest of braves in this fire-fighting game."
What? Never a one?? Oh, It's really a shame
That no-one would dare to put out Denzil's flame.

Then suddenly one little boy said "I'll go!
I'm not scared of dragons, I'll have you all know.
I'll tell him exactly what's here in my mind,
I think that inside, he's a scaredey-cat kind!"

With that he set off to do battle I think.
But quick as a flash, and as quick as a wink,
Denzil appeared, spouting flames from his cave.
Oh, quite the unfriendly-est way to behave.

Our brave little hero just stood there and said
"I'm not scared of you, 'cos I'm young Fearless Fred!
It's naughty to tamper with matches and fire.
There's only one lesson that you now require."

So he picked up a bucket of water nearby
And poured it right over that dragon! Oh my!!
But strange as it seems, Denzil didn't get cross.
He looked rather pleased that his flames he'd now lost.

"Oh, thank you young Fred. Now my nose can cool down.
And please tell your friends living down in the town
That now I feel cooler, My bad temper's gone.
We'll all live together, Be friends from now on!

"Naughty Edward!"

Edward the Elf has been naughty again.
Teasing the Butterflies down in the lane.
Hiding himself, in the way that Elves do,
Then waiting to pounce out. And give a loud 'BOO'

Elves should be caring, not naughty, they say.
But Edward, he's different in most every way.
Sticking his tongue out, and cheeky as well,
Oh, what will become of him! No-one can tell.

Now, Oswald the Owl sitting high in his tree
Is the wisest of owls, and said "Leave it to me.
I'll give it great thought, and I'll think of a plan
To change the bad ways of this naughty young man."

Poor Butterflies, frightened what Edward might do
Were all of a-flutter, were all of a stew!
Cos someone had seen a sight ne're to forget.
That naughty boy elf, with a BUTTERFLY NET !!!

"He's going to catch us" they cried with alarm.
"He's going to catch us, and do us great harm.
Caught in a butterfly net of all things,
Could quite ruin our day, and could damage our wings"

That Edward! He sat on a leaf with his net
Waiting and hoping a catch he would get.
Not knowing that Oswald the Owl was around
Till suddenly 'Whoosh!' Oswald swooped to the ground.

It made Edward jump, and he slipped off his leaf.
Then tumbled head first in that net spread beneath.
When, quick as a wink Oswald hooted with glee,
Flew off, with that net filled with Elf, up the tree.

Edward yelled "Help" He was frightened alright.
Swept high up a tree to a dizzying height.
Laying all of a heap in that butterfly net
Was something I'm sure he will never forget.

The Owl glared at Edward, and said "Now my son,
Just think of the damage you might well have done.
Netting a Butterfly's not the done thing!
You might well have damaged its delicate wing."

"I'm sure YOU were scared to be caught in that net.
All tangled and twisted, your feet 'round your neck.
I'll take you back down to be safe on the floor,
If you promise that you won't be bad any more.

A lesson well learned on the way to behave.
Our Elf listened well to the message Owl gave.
He said "Cross my heart, I'll be good from now on"
Owl nodded his head, Swooped them down

AND WAS GONE!!

"Must it Rain?"

Rain, Rain, Go away.
And let the sun come out today.
Oh how can I go out and play
When every cloud's a gloomy grey.

Rain, Rain, Go away!
Today I am on holiday.
I've learned my numbers, letters too,
To spoil my fun's unkind of you.

Rain, Rain, Can't you see
I am as cross as cross can be!
They say it's too wet to go out.
Though I've got wellies, firm and stout.

Rain, Rain, Go away.
And please be off without delay.
Yes, please be gone within the hour,
And let this be a passing shower.

Rain, Rain, Falling down
O'er the village, o'er the town.
On my window-pane I see
Drops running down like tears for me.

Rain! Rain!! Can it be
You heard, and listened to my plea?
Because I see up there on high,
A RAINBOW, FILLING ALL THE SKY.

AAAHHH!!!!
SV19

"What Did I do?

I don't think Dad was very pleased
When I helped dig up his weeds.
I didn't know they'd turn to flowers,
That he'd spent planting out for hours.

He didn't thank me. Not a bit
For digging him that great big pit.
He yelled a lot, jumped up and down
Just like a toy that's over-wound!

How could I know his seeding bed
Was something special. No-one said!
He threatened that he'd box my ears
For sharpening up his secateurs.

I only pruned the raspberry bed
And other stick things that looked dead.
Ever seen a grown man cry?
I have. Don't know the reason why.

Perhaps he didn't like me squeeze
A pathway through the beans and peas!
Those nasty twig things that they climb
Stuck in my leg. And in my behind.

I threw them in a great big pile.
That somehow made my dad grow wild!
He roared "The garden's out of bounds!!"
Don't think he likes me hanging 'round.

My help's not needed any more.
I'll go and help the man next door!

"Busy Barry Bee"

Barry the Bee
Was out buzzing along
Humming his favourite
Sing-a-long-song.
A song about primroses,
Buttercups, spring;
Bout warm sunny days,
And the harvest they bring.

The Queen Bee you see
From her Throne-Room had said
That all of her subjects,
(Including you Fred)
Should work extra hard
Gathering pollen that day,
As a big special order
Had just come their way.

A nice little girl
(Listen please, won't you Fred)
Had got a sore throat,
And a cold in the head.
Her Doctor prescribed
That the best cure would be
A hot drink of Honey,
To have with her tea.

So Barry the Bee
And his friends all agreed

That this little girl
With a sore throat would need
Plenty of honey.
So away they all sped,
a-buzzing and busy, yes,
(and that means you Fred)

The cure was miraculous,
Certain, and sure.
The honey delicious,
Oh, need I say more?
While Barry and friends
Are tired out, and in bed.
Who's snoring the loudest?
You've got it. Fat Fred!

"Derek The Dinosaur"

Derek the Dinosaur ambled along
Singing a sad little Dinosaur song.
Singing a song that was terribly old,
Much older than Dinosaur's, so I've been told.

The words of this song caused poor Derek to cry.
I feel almost certain you're going to ask 'Why?'
Because it for-told of a terrible end
For Dinosaur Derek, And all of his friends.

Now all of this happened a long time ago.
Even before I was born. Yes, that's so!
Back when the world was quite young, and quite new.
I know Derek's song. Shall I tell it to you?

"You Dinosaurs think You're important and smart.
That here in the world you all play a big part.
But hark to this warning I bring loud and clear
One bright sunny morning, you'll all disappear!"

The rest of the Dinosaurs laughed, said 'No way!
We rule all the earth, and we're planning to stay.
No-one can touch us, we're big, and we're strong'
But as we all know, they were terribly wrong.

Our Derek thought That's not the way to behave.
I think I'll go live in a nice high-up cave!
Down on the plains it's as clear as can be
You wouldn't be safe from a 'Ca-Tas-Tro-Phe!!'

Well, tragedy happened, as you're well aware.
The sun lost its brightness, 'twas dark everywhere.
And Dinosaurs vanished. Might never have been.
They vanished alright. Never more to be seen.

But Derek was safe in his cave near the sky.
He lived there for millions of years. Would I lie?
Would I tell fibs? Tell you porkies I ask?
No! Derek was King as long centuries passed.

Then one day a man who was walking his dog
Sought shelter away from a very thick fog.
Found Derek's cave, and discovered quite soon
That this was indeed Derek's own living-room.

"I've found me a Dinosaur!" Cried this nice man.
"I'll take it home with me as soon as I can.
It must be so lonely, up here in this cave.
We'll prove, yes we will, that one Dinosaur's saved!!"

Well! There Derek stands for the whole world to see.
So proud of the fact he's called 'Pre-History'
I saw him again, 'twas just last week I think.
I gave him a smile, he looked back, and he winked!!

Poor Derek!"

Derek the Dinosaur's terribly sad.
He sits all alone, Oh, the poor little lad.
Never a sound near his cave way up high.
Our Dinosaur wipes a lone tear from his eye.

"Nobody loves me" he sniffled and said,
"If it wasn't so early, I'd go back to bed!!
I wish, oh I wish that somebody would call."
But nobody answered. No, no-one at all.

Now why should poor Derek feel lonely and blue?
Cos Dinosaurs rule all the world. Yes, that's true.
They can go places that we've never been.
From plains to high mountains ... And bits in between.

Can just pack their bag, and be off in a trice.
No passports to bother them, isn't that nice?
No tickets to buy, all those bookings to make.
It couldn't be easier, for goodness sake.

No, that's not the answer to Derek's distress.
I has to be something more serious, I guess.
It's not very often that Dinosaurs cry,
So what is the matter? What's causing him to sigh?

"Today is my one special day in the year,"
Sobbed Derek, in tones not too easy to hear.
"When friends should call 'round from all points on the earth
To show that they know it's the date of my birth!"

"It's my birthday! And nobody's sent me a card.
No presents to open. Oh, isn't life hard?
You'd think they'd be pleased that I've managed to be
Still running around at a million -and-three!!"

How thoughtless! Unfeeling!! How really unkind!!!
If you had been there, you'd have spoken your mind.
Poor Derek, no party with games to enjoy,
Small wonder he felt such an unhappy boy.

But suddenly such a strange sound filled the air.
The oddest of music. But coming from where?
When out through the mists came a procession so grand,
And all being led by a Dinosaur Band.

They hadn't forgotten! The crowds grew and grew.
Whilst all of them sang 'Happy Birthday To You'
Such presents and cards, and a huge birthday cake.
The largest the Dinosaur baker could bake.

And so in the end everything came out right.
Derek the Dinosaur's filled with delight.
The party went on the whole night so 'tis said.
I know you weren't there. You were tucked up in bed.

"Wonderful Wizard"

Now, Willy the Wiz, as I'm sure you've heard tell
Is exceedingly good at the weaving of spells.
There, way up in his room at the top of the tower
He sits working his magic for hours and hours.

Magic that makes all our lives spin around.
The cause and the reason, before never found.
But Willie the Wizard wields power, I must say,
To make all things happen to us every day.

He looks up your number, and if you've been good,
Behaved in the manner you know that you should,
Then Willy will smile. Wave his wand, and he'll say
"I'll magic up sunshine to brighten your day"

But if you've been bad, oh dear, then I'm afraid
A quite different sort of a spell will be made.
"You deserve nothing but grey skies" he'll say.
Here's thunder and lightning to ruin your day"

Be it snowing or blowing, and everyone's wet,
Or a hot sunny day that you'll never forget,
Whatever the weather, whatever you crave,
It all now depends on the way you behave.

SV19

Oh, such is the power of this great Wizard man.
Have things happened to you that you don't understand?
Strange happenings, that you thought were
just merely chance.
That you'd soon forget. Not worth one second glance.

But Willy the Wizard is watching, to see
If you are as nice as you surely can be.
You'll heed him of course, Oh, I'm sure you'll agree,
Cos Willy the Wizard's none other than ... ME.

"Ronnie the Cat"

Ronnie the cat
Is exceedingly fat,
Is as round as a bouncy balloon.
All day lays in the sun
Whilst his bulging black tum
Is likely to burst pretty soon.

But Ronnie the cat
Is quite well aware that
The birds in the trees seem to know
He's too bulky to jump,
Just a big, bumpy lump, who's
Movements are terribly slow!

So they twitter and tease,
Hop around as they please.
But Ronnie pretends not to care.
Simply closes his eyes,
Fall asleep, they surmise.
But Ronnie, is fully aware.

He keeps quiet and still,
Hardly breathing, until with
A yowl, and a howl! Goodness me!!
Did he bounce like a ball?
Who can tell, can recall
How he shot to the top of the tree.

But the tree's very high,
Almost reaches the sky,
Poor Ronnie is stuck, and held fast.
Till a Fireman, with ladder
Sorts out the sad matter.
Shamed Ronnie is rescued at last.

So what use is a cat
That is terribly fat, though
Quite handsome, I'm sure you'll agree.
Oh, the answer is clear,
And it's happening right here.
Ronnie purrs, never stirs from my knee.

"A mountain of ..."

Miss. Dora Dormouse stepped out her front door.
A thing she had done countless mornings before.
But instead of the view that she knew oh, so well
Was a big blob of yellow, with a strange, haunting smell.

"That's very annoying" she said "Tell me, why
Has my world turned bright yellow, and where is the sky!
It's really quite odd to a poor timid mouse
To find a big blob there. As big as my house!"

"And how did it get here. Oh, what a to-do.
To have a big yellow thing blocking your view.
It's right on my doorstep. That's not very nice.
To move it away, needs an army of mice"

She gave it a prod with her walking-stick cane.
She gave it another. Again and again.
It didn't protest, make a sound, even cry;
D'you know why it didn't? No? Neither do I!

But Miss. Dora Dormouse, a clever old girl,
She looked at it closely, her mind in a whirl.
"If that really is what I think it might be,
I'll take a small sample, to have with my tea.

It was what she thought. What a lovely surprise.
From that new 'Mousey Lottery' Was it first prize?
Dora phoned all her friends, and they flocked round to see
What could pass as a mountain of CHEESE easily.

So they partied and ate. And they partied and ate.
The whole month of July they would never forget.
And me? I'm so glad now that I hadn't stopped
To pick up that nice bit of Cheddar I'd dropped.

"Miss Dora's revenge"

Edward the elf has been naughty again.
The King of the elves said "That boy is a pain.
He really could be such a nice little lad,
But his recent behavior is driving us mad."

"He's frightened the fishes that swim in the sea,
Disturbed all the birds nesting up in the tree.
While Miss. Dora Dormouse ... don't talk about that!
Naughty Edward pretended that he was a cat."

He watched and he waited outside her front door,
From a place that he must have done often before.
And when timid Dora stepped out, oh, I vow
From the bushes beyond came a fearsome ME-OW!!

"A Cat! It's a Cat!! Dora cried in alarm.
As a poor timid Dormouse, it could do me harm.
Oh, save me, please save me, oh dear deary me.
He'll catch me, and barbecue me for his tea"

Wicked Edward kept howling and yowling like mad;
But soon got his comeuppance, for which I am glad.
Miss. Dora decided to be very brave.
You do, when you've got your own life to be saved.

She picked up the garden hose that was quite near,
Though trembling a little she conquered her fear,
Then, aiming it at a convenient gap
She plucked up her courage, and turned on the tap!

WOOSH went the water like a downpour of rain.
WOOSH went the water, again and again.
That stopped his yowling. It stopped it like that.
Cos Edward now looked like a drowned pussy-cat.

So if you set out on a practical joke,
Remember these words that a wise man once spoke.
"Better by far that you share a good laugh.
Or maybe like Edward, you'll get a cold bath!"

And so our book
Has reached its end.
I hope that we've
Become good friends,
That you've enjoyed
Those that you've met,
Like Dora Dormouse.
Oh, don't forget
Naughty Edward,
Winnie Witch,
And all the others
Warm and rich.
Their stories may,
'Could be' we'll say
Come back again
Another day.
And so, until perhaps
They do, I'll just say
"Bye now, Toodle-oo!"